Today I'm Going Fishing with My Dad

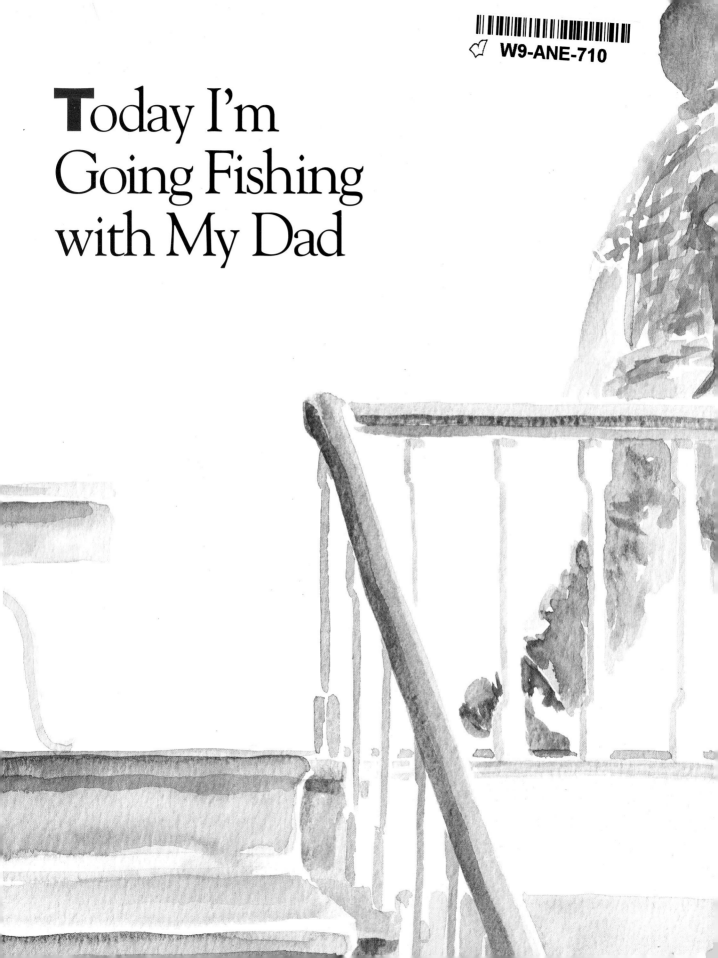

Today I'm Going Fishing with My Dad

Story by **N.L. Sharp**

Pictures by **Chris L. Demarest**

Boyds Mills Press

Published by Caroline House

Boyds Mills Press, Inc.

A Highlights Company

815 Church Street

Honesdale, Pennsylvania 18431

Printed in **China**

Publisher Cataloging-in-Publication Data

Sharp, N.L.

   Today I'm going fishing with my Dad / by N.L. Sharp ; illustrated by
Chris L. Demarest. — 1st ed.

[32]p. : col. ill. ; cm.

Summary : A young boy remembers what it is like to go fishing with his father.

Hardcover ISBN 1-56397-107-0   Paperback ISBN 1-56397-613-7

1. Family life — Juvenile fiction. 2. Fathers — Juvenile fiction.

[1. Family life. 2. Fathers.] I. Demarest, Chris L., ill. II. Title.

   [E] — dc20   1993

Library of Congress Catalog Card Number 92-73994

Book designed by Joy Chu

The text of this book is set in 24-point Nicholas Cochin.

The illustrations are done in watercolors.

Hardcover 10 9 8 7 6 5 4 3

Softcover 10 9 8 7 6 5 4

For my mother and father with love

–N. L. S.

To Liz and *P*eter

–C.L.D.

T oday I'm going fishing with my dad.

We spent all day yesterday getting ready to go. We dug the fishing poles and the tackle box out of the closet. I practiced casting in the driveway, while Dad sorted through the junk in the old red box.

"I don't know what happened to all those hooks
and bobbers I bought last year. Looks like we'll
have to pick up some more at the lake," he said, just as
he does every year when he cleans out the tackle box for
our first fishing trip of the season.

We dug around under the basement steps until we found the camping stools and Dad's old black wading boots. The left boot has a large hole in the toe, but Dad never seems to notice that. "My lucky fishing boots! Just what I need to keep my feet dry," he cried.

We loaded all of the fishing gear into the trunk of the car, and then it was time for bed. "We need to be up at the crack of dawn," Dad said. "The early bird catches the worm, you know."

Sure enough, Dad was right. Bright and early this morning, we were out in the backyard, digging for worms. And we caught one. Just one, though.

"That's okay," Dad said as we headed back to the house. "We can pick up some more at the lake."

Mom was still sleeping, so Dad quietly fixed breakfast, while I made our picnic lunch. I packed all of Dad's favorites. Peanut-butter-and-pickle sandwiches, potato chips, and raisin-oatmeal cookies.

"Eat up," Dad said as he put my eggs and toast down in front of me. "A man gets mighty hungry while he's waiting for the fish to bite."

Now, at last, we're off, bouncing along the old

gravel road that leads down to the water's edge.

"An adventure," Dad says.
"Men's day out," Dad says.
"Just you, me, and the fish," Dad says.
"Great," I say.

"Can't wait," I say.

"When do we get to the lake?" I say. But silently I'm thinking...*I hate going fishing with my dad.*

The mosquitoes buzz around my head and bite me on the arms and legs, and **I** always come back with ten new places that need scratching.

I have to be so quiet. *I* can only talk in a whisper, and then only if *I* have something really important to say, like "*D*ad, *I* think *I* have a nibble" or "*D*ad, *I* have to go to the bathroom real bad."

I hate getting the worms out of the can so that Dad can bait our hooks. They wiggle and squirm, and right when I think I finally have one, it always manages to slip right through my fingers.

I can never get my line cast right. It's always catching in a tree or on a log or in the weeds. Once I even got the hook caught in the back of my shirt.

The sun beats down on me, making sweat run down my face and neck and back.

I'm always hungry, and there is never anything to eat but peanut-butter-and-pickle sandwiches, soggy potato chips, and raisin-oatmeal cookies.

I have to go to the bathroom in the trees!

And that's not even the worst part. The worst part comes when I actually catch a fish. It jumps and bumps and wiggles as Dad takes it off the hook and attaches it to the stringer, and I have to sit next to it for the rest of the day.

*Then, when the day is over, and we finally get to go home, **I** have to eat fish for supper. **I** hate eating fish for supper.*

*But **I** love spending time with my dad, and my dad likes to go fishing, so…*

...today I'm going fishing with my dad.